Enid Blyton™

TOYLAND™ STORIES

MR PLOD AND THE SORE ARM

This edition first published in Great Britain by HarperCollins Publishers Ltd in 1998

1 3 5 7 9 10 8 6 4 2

Copyright © 1998 Enid Blyton Company Ltd. Enid Blyton's signature mark and the words 'NODDY' and 'TOYLAND' are Registered Trade Marks of Enid Blyton Ltd. For further information on Enid Blyton please contact www.blyton.com

ISBN: 0 00 136081 7

Cover design and illustrations by County Studio

Printed and bound in Singapore.

Enid Blyton™

TOYLAND™ STORIES

MR PLOD AND THE SORE ARM

Collins

An Imprint of HarperCollins*Publishers*

Mr Plod was riding along one morning, when...

CRASH!

...His bike hit a stone, and poor Mr Plod went flying.
"Ouch!" cried Mr Plod. "My arm!"

Big-Ears ran out of his house to help Mr Plod.
"You'll need to rest that arm for a few days," he
said, putting it in a sling. "Try not to move it at all!"
Mr Plod snorted. "Rest?" he said. "And what will
happen to Toy Town if I rest?
There will be mayhem
without a policeman
on duty!"

Mr Plod got up to leave. "Thank you for the sling, Big-Ears - now I must get back to work!" he said.

Once in Toy Town, he bumped into Noddy.

"Ouch!" said Mr Plod. Even with the sling, his arm was still very sore.

"Just the person I was hoping to see!" cried Noddy. "Oh - what have you done to your arm?"

Mr Plod coughed. "Nothing a policeman can't handle!" he said. "Now, what's the problem?"

"Someone has climbed through my window and stolen some biscuits!" said Noddy. "But... are you sure you will be able to help? Perhaps you should be resting your arm?"

"Nonsense!" said Mr Plod sternly. "Now then, tell me everything you can about this terrible biscuit-stealing, Noddy, and I'll take down some notes."

But Mr Plod found that he was not able to take down any notes. The hand he used for writing was now in a sling. He couldn't hold his pencil!

"No matter, no matter," said Mr Plod quickly.
"We'll go straight to your house so I can search
for clues."

Mr Plod did not need to search for clues, however. As they were approaching Noddy's house, they saw the biscuit-thief climbing through Noddy's window. He had come back for more biscuits.

"Ah, so it's you!" Mr Plod exclaimed as the biscuit-thief crept back out of the window. "Gobbo, the goblin! Hold out your arms, my lad, so I can handcuff you. You're under arrest!"

Mr Plod's handcuffs were in his back pocket and he quickly tried to reach them. But he found that he could not. He needed his right arm to reach the handcuffs, and his right arm was now in a sling! "Quick, he's getting away!" Noddy cried, as Gobbo made a run for it.

"Blow your whistle so someone stops him, Mr Plod!"

But Mr Plod found that he could not reach his whistle either.

"Oh, you've let him get away, Mr Plod!" Noddy sighed crossly. "What use is a policeman with an arm in a sling? You might as well go off duty until your arm is better!"

Still very cross, Noddy marched off to his house to see if Gobbo had left any of his biscuits. Mr Plod marched off too. But he was not going off duty.

"There's traffic directing to do," he told himself, adopting one of his important-looking frowns. "There'll be all sorts of accidents if I'm not there to help."

Reaching the centre of Toy Town, Mr Plod stood in the middle of the road. He waited for some vehicles to appear so he could direct them. He liked it best when two vehicles came at once so he could let one go and make the other stop.

The other thing he liked was when a car was coming but someone wanted to cross the road. He would make the car grind to a halt by raising his arm!

"Ah, there's Mr Wobbly Man wanting to cross the road at this very moment," Mr Plod said to himself with a smile.

"And here's Mr Sparks approaching in his truck. I'll make Mr Sparks stop so Mr Wobbly Man can cross safely."

Mr Plod tried to raise his arm, but he had forgotten that there was a sling on the arm he always used to direct traffic.

Fortunately, Mr Wobbly Man was just able to jump out of the way in time. But it meant that he was wobbling all over the place.
He was very cross.

"You're meant to protect us pedestrians, Mr Plod!" he cried. "Now I'll be wobbling like this for the rest of the day!"

Mr Plod was not listening to him, however.
He had spotted another car coming
towards him. It was
Noddy's!

Then he heard someone coming
from the other direction, ringing a
bell. It was Big-Ears on his bicycle!

"I'd better make sure they don't collide," Mr Plod said to himself in a bit of a panic. "I'll wave Big-Ears through with one arm and make Noddy stop with the other arm."

Then Mr Plod remembered. "No, I can't do that," he said. "One arm is in a sling. I'll have to try and do the waving through and the stopping with the *same* arm!"

Poor Mr Plod got himself in a right muddle. He twisted to left and right. Then to right and left. Noddy and Big-Ears really could not follow his directions at all.

Noddy and Big-Ears drove right into each other!

Noddy and Big-Ears were very cross. "Please go home, Mr Plod, until you can take that arm out of its sling!" they shouted.

"But Toy Town can't manage without me!" protested Mr Plod. Then he looked at their faces. "Well. Maybe just for a day or so, then..."

Get well soon, Mr Plod!

THE NODDY CLASSIC LIBRARY
by Enid Blyton™

Available in hardback
Published by HarperCollins